THE TRUE STORY OF
DICK WHITTINGTON

THE TRUE STORY OF DICK WHITTINGTON

A CHRISTMAS STORY FOR CAT-LOVERS

BY

OSBERT SITWELL

LONDON
HOME & VAN THAL LTD.
3 CLIFFORD STREET. W.1

First Published 1945

The story which follows first appeared in Horizon and is now
presented in a revised form

Printed by THE CHASETON PRESS of H. WILLIAMS & SON LTD.,
222 Grays Inn Road, London, W.C.1

YOU may well inquire, child, the history and purpose of that enormous red-brick building over there; that is the famous *Whittington Central Cats' Aid Society and Sanatorium*. And, for once, I will consent to tell you its story, on condition that you do not interrupt and that if you fail to understand anything, either a word or sentiment, you will keep your questions until the end. I do it all the more readily because it is a tale that will help to equip you for the world. In order, however, that you may derive the full benefit from the moral to be drawn, we must begin almost at the end, so that we may obtain thereby a glimpse of the glories that crowned Whittington's career, because it is essentially, in the delightful modern phrase, which you would do well to ponder, a 'success-story,' indicating how Perseverance and Industry are rewarded, and that we need never despair of Providence assisting us, if only, at the beginning of our lives, we learn to assist ourselves.

*   *   *   *

It was a typical November, early November, day in the City of London. All the morning the crowds had surged in the streets, as they still called the narrow traffic lanes between the camouflaged hoardings that hide the broken façades of houses and the derelict brick-strewn areas. Here and there, a stout Norman tower survived, or an opalescent belfry by Wren pricked the grey sky as it had done for three centuries, while from it sounded the accustomed peals. The excited people jostled one another, and in places the crowd was so great that it broke through the hoardings and swarmed into the bomb craters, now, by the miracles of Science, as large as Greek theatres. Throughout the morning the weather had been fine, and not *really* cold, the onlookers had said as they thrashed their arms together and blew their noses. It only *seemed* cold, because this year the Show had taken so long a time to pass. But that was natural enough, too, and one must not grumble, for it had been designed to portray the Blessings of Peace.

As usual, the Bishops had blessed the tanks, that were wreathed with branches of olive, and in short sermons had pointed out that if men wanted peace, they must avoid being *peaceable*, must on the contrary, be prepared to fight everywhere, everyone, at once, and at the same time. Peace was not something negative, not just a period in which people were not making war; it should be a period of active preparation for the next war. Only thus could a true peace be attained ; only thus should we make ourselves worthy of peace. . . . Then the procession started. First, on a mammoth car, came the miniature model of a bombed city — easy to make, but effective. (The onlookers cheered themselves hoarse.) Then followed bodies of flame-throwers in masks and armour, who drew behind them on a carrier a vast bomb, then bits of aircraft, lifted shoulder-high, then detachments of atom-splitters and electron-smashers in their uniforms of synthetic rubber, then platoons of freezers in their new, non-conductive suits, inflated like those of divers, then a car on which were placed what the crowd for the most part held to be dummies, copied from the enemy dead— but some maintained that this would be too expensive, and that they were the real thing, preserved by a new secret process—and, finally, battalions of the new peace-keepers, as they are termed, wound up the whole parade, their faces painted with pigs' blood, while, for arms, they carried knives, bombs, grenades, pocket machine-guns, rays, and rubber truncheons. These last were the most popular item of all, and the crowd, especially the school-boys in it, cheered till they could cheer no more. But everyone had enjoyed the Show. It had struck a new note, people agreed ; you know, *modern, realistic ;* none of the old papier-mâché stuff. Alas, as the Lord Mayor's coach, in which that dignitary, with fur lined robe and cocked hat, and the Lady Mayoress could be seen rolling like porpoises, neared the spectators, a drizzle began and a little marred the pageantry.

The afternoon was wet, very wet, the rain pouring down the folds of thousands of waterproof coats, seeming to make of their shapes something noble, as if turning them to stone. Lamps glowed through the yellow darkness, and the reflecting surfaces of wet, broken stone, wet, broken tarmac, wet, broken cement, showed an infinity of watery lights. The faces of the newspaper boys, as they dashed along the pavements, were turned at that angle towards the sky, at which the faces of figure-heads are set, and were varnished with the rain.

'*Lord Mayor's Banquet, Sensation!*' they were crying. The eager purchasers obstructed the swift darting of their progress, bringing them to a halt, and pennies clinked quickly in scabbed hands. '*Sensation! Sudden Illness of Lord Mayor!*'

In the Guildhall, under the lights, the tables had looked magnificent. The note of peace, which had pervaded and animated the Show, was carried right through the whole conception of the banquet, and great bunches of orchids, mauve and rose or spotted and stippled like snakes, were arranged in vases that were facsimiles of the most popular kinds of shell and bomb, but fashioned in gold plate. In the centre stood a golden skull, made into a loving cup ; a replica of the cranium of the executed chief of the enemy nation. This beautiful piece of work was a gift from the Mayors of the principal cities of our Allies. The guests had spilled turtle soup down their red, voracious gullets ; roast beef had followed, after soles ; sorbets, quails, ices, grapes in jewelled bunches, sweets, all had gone down the same scarlet path. Now came the toasts and, best of all, the speeches. The Prime Minister of the day stood up, to couple the name of the Lord Mayor with Peace and Democracy.

'The vast panorama of peace,' he had begun, 'which has been so ably, so ingeniously, translated for us into terms of pageantry today, is indeed an inspiring an—em —er—almost an intimidating prospect. Across the water, now, no enemy exists. World-famed empires have been thrust down beneath the mire of the centuries, and cities of a legendary renown and beauty have been erased, or, in the more amiable term of one of our great allies, liquidated. (Laughter.) This is an achievement of which all who shared in it may well be proud. And in it, no one has better played his part than the old, and I am glad to say, the new (cries of hear, hear!) Lord Mayor. You know him here, in this great City of London—I know him, as he was to us, in his private capacity during the hour of the nation's need. He is a great killer! (Tremendous applause.) The complicated and wonderful killing machines, which his genius has shaped, and his indomitable energy produced, are second to none. Though it may be said—and it is high praise!—that in a world where every international effort has seemed doomed to failure, the great armament firms alone have set an example of successful co-operation, yet he has shown himself a patriot, first and foremost, willing to slaughter all who bar the nation's progress. But you know him: you may well be proud of him ; I need say no more, except that his example must inspire us.

'The ideals of Europe, those ideals of Christianity, of brotherly love and chivalry, which raised the great cathedrals, have seldom been better exemplified than in the laying low of these same edifices. Our ideals have won through, and we stand on the threshold of a new world. It is in many ways, in most ways, a far, far better world than the old ; but it will not be—oh no!—an easy world. But I have never promised you easy things. In the old days, after we had fought, we lived by trade ; but now the extermination of our chief customers has rendered us independent of them. Instead we must live by insuring each other's washing, which we must increasingly take in. But, Your Royal Highnesses, Your Excellencies, my lords, ladies and gentlemen, what is the lesson—the lesson that we must learn and treasure in our hearts, if not in our heads, from henceforth? (Pause.) That we must be true to ourselves (outburst of stamping)—to ourselves, I was saying ; that we must steel our hearts, in the sacred cause of Equality and Free Speech to kill everyone who does not agree with us (prolonged cheering), so that another war may be unthinkable, and so that men, pacific at heart as the beasts of the field, the forest and the jungle, may enjoy in peace those blessings which they deserve. But we are not revengeful—oh no! Nor, as I can prove, are we selfish. For a war, out of which we gain no material advantage, must be as unselfish and praiseworthy as, judged by the standard of statesmanship, it is wise. The Little Man, now master, entered this war from no motive of the head, but of the heart. And feeling is a more noble process than thinking—and more democratic : for everyone can feel, but not everybody can think (cheers). Otherwise I should not be addressing you here today, for there are sterner tasks to which I should attend. In the Peace before you, I offer you no period of slothful ease (cheers), no time for talk or reflection (stamping). It must be an epoch of endeavour, of strife (tremendous applause), of sweat (roars and cheering), of keeping your nose to the grindstone (tumultuous cheers, and waving of handkerchiefs): it must be,—And in this manner the great oration tottered inexorably to its appointed anticlimax.

Then, after it had ended, and after the storm of cheering had subsided, the toastmaster knocked again on the table with his gavel, and called out in a ceremonial voice, tinged by its accustomed burden of superiority:

'Your Royal Highnesses, Your Excellencies, my lords, ladies and gentlemen, pray silence for the Lord Mayor elect of the City of London, now entering on his third term of office: Sir Richard Whittington!!!'

The new Lord Mayor, his own successor, stood up, and with a singular ease of manner and appearance of spontaneity, began his speech. All that day he had felt ill, but no one would have known it: nor could he himself make out quite what was the matter, suffering, as he did, some uneasy stirring of the heart for which, perhaps, modern doctors have not yet found a name. As when a serious illness begins, so everything seemed strange, and the senses, each one, sight, taste, sound, hearing and touch seemed to translate the messages they received differently from their wont—especially hearing. Even the pealing of the chimes of bells now ringing to announce his third span, carried for him an echo difficult to seize, some refrain of words heard long ago. At times he almost caught their drift. '*Turn Again,*' he thought he could distinguish—but it must have been very long ago. Meanwhile, he was making his speech, and so could not give full attention to the other matter. And he was speaking well. ('*Turn Again*'!).

People liked to hear what he was saying, and Lady Whittington, from the end of the table, was watching him intently. Dressed in black velvet, it was the emerald ring she wore on her finger that first drew one's attention— and no wonder, for it was the Whittington Emerald, as it is known, one of the largest, and of the most pure and vivid quality in the world. (It had been acquired for Sir Richard many years before in Tongador.) But, in any case, with her white hair, and her skin, like white kid, she was a handsome woman, especially at first sight. It was as though she had been specially created to glow with a white radiance at public functions, the whiteness being there to show off the jewels, as the hoar-frost on a Christmas tree is designed to set off the toys and tinsel. But then, after having just accepted this conclusion, one realised that, after all, the rime was genuine, thrown off by the inner core, rather than the deposit of the years.

For so tall, imposing a person, she was well finished except for her hands, which looked like a sketch for hands, curiously lumpy, too, so that when she took off her long, fawn-coloured gloves it was as though she were peeling potatoes. With her large eyes, earth-brown, she continued to scan her husband's face, and in them shone a certain anxiety ; no doubt she knew that he had been feeling ill.

He spoke admirably ; a full ten minutes passed before he came to his chief theme, the gratitude that the nation, the Empire, the world, and those of the conquered even more than of the conquering powers, owed to the man who had just spoken. 'Gratitude,' he was saying, 'is perhaps the first, the most typical and important of human qualities, and it is one that the Little Man possesses in the lowest—I use "lowest" in its new democratic sense, meaning "highest" (a word that itself reeks of the prejudices of the bad old days)—in the lowest degree. The good faith of the crowd—and what is the crowd, but a herd?—I mean an august assemblage—of Little Men, has long been proverbial as that of princes. But gratitude must not only be felt, it must be expressed, expressed for a lifetime. And how can this quality, this gratitude, best be expressed?' . . . Here Sir Richard fell silent, to mark the end of one of the periods of his speech, no less than to allow a time for the burst of applause which this sonorous display of sentiment naturally promoted, partly to spend itself. As it began to die, he lifted up a hand in the style of the great orators to quell it. A profound silence of anticipation interposed, in which sounded a faint, sad mewing. Lady Whittington heard it, and looked over her shoulder. Her husband meanwhile was proceeding with his speech. 'Gratitude,' he was saying, 'gratitude—' but at this moment a gaunt, hungry-looking, rather mangy black cat, with wild and haunted eyes, jumped on to the table, and turned its whiskered, grizzled face towards him.

The cat stole the limelight. On it the gaze of every guest was fixed, as it stalked towards the Lord Mayor, so delicately threading its way among the orchids and gold plate. It was not, perhaps, really so unusual a cat, nor so old in its aspect as one might have presumed. It was not so much unlike the ordinary run—if one may use the word in that connection—of cats; it even resembled many cats that can be seen flickering in figures-of-eight through railings, or leaping vertically, with the dynamism of ecstasy, up tree-trunks, or up high walls to the beloved roof-tops, their dominion of the night. Nevertheless, when you looked, the cat *was* old, ancient more than old. . . . Now it had come so near the Lord Mayor, that it rubbed its neck against his hand. 'Gratitude,' he stammered with pale lips, 'Gratitude' . . . and then, with a moan, fell back. The cat, seeming much concerned, jumped with grace and agility—considering its age—on to the floor, and nestled against him. The mewing turned to a loud contented purr. . . . Along the tables, there was an uneasy stirring of hands and eyes, and a few guests, with less restraint than their fellows, murmured 'So it *is* true. The man's haunted by a cat!' . . . The Lord Mayor was carried out into the air, Lady Whittington followed him, and the guests dispersed.

For several days he was confined to his bed, and could see no one. But since the incident had aroused public interest, Lady Whittington allowed herself to be interviewed by members of the Press. She began, with considerable charm, to explain that Sir Richard was, and always had been—*always* was the word upon which she lingered—particularly devoted to animals, though she must confess that he preferred dogs to cats. His Sealyham, 'Tufts,' was his constant companion, and she had often heard Sir Richard say that he did not know how he would have got through the war without the doggies. But, though he favoured dogs, he had done more for cats than any man living. He had founded first *The*

Whittington Central Cats' Aid Society and Sanatorium; a place to which old cats could retire in comfort, where they could be well looked after, watched and tended, not allowed to stray, and where they could be sure, too, of their saucer of milk at regular intervals. But though this rest-house served, and continued to serve, a useful purpose, it was situated in too noisy and central a district to obtain the best results. It was very tempting for cats. So Sir Richard had then planned and endowed *The Cats' Charterhouse,* in the grounds of Whittington, the family seat in Gloucestershire, and finally, since that. too, failed to meet the need, he had inaugurated *The Cats' Provident Society Almshouse* in the Outer Hebrides.

All this work, into which had gone so much forethought and imagination, he had achieved for cats, though, in this resembling many gallant and eminent men before him—Lord Roberts and Lord Kitchener for example—he was, as ordinary people termed it, *afraid* of cats; this apparent fear of them, however, was not a phobia, but to be attributed to what was now a recognised illness, termed by doctors 'Cat-asthma.' He was, in fact, allergic to cats as certain other men are to hay-seed or some kinds of scented soap. And the war had aggravated his sufferings in this respect. It had taken its toll of him. Even if the Prime Minister himself at the Guildhall Banquet had not borne such eloquent testimony to the patriotism of her husband, the citizens, the Corporation and the Sheriffs had done so in practical fashion by their insistence on his retaining for a third span the office of Lord Mayor of London.

At this point a particularly impudent journalist had interrupted with the question:

'All the same, m'lady, wouldn't it be the truth to state that Sir Richard owed his fortune in the first place to a cat?'

Lady Whittington did not allow herself to be disturbed or distressed by the singular lack of feeling shown by this man. She replied in a steady and decisive voice:

'My husband owes his position to his talents, his application, and his unremitting zeal for the Public Weal.'

*　　　*　　　*　　　*

The origin of Dick Whittington was, and still is, a little obscure. Some aver that he came from Whittington in Gloucestershire, but I hold that he only settled there when he had made his fortune, and that he hailed originally—and all the neighbourhood agrees with me—from Whittington in Derbyshire. It is a comfortable enough little place now. Trams clank down the road between lines of red council-houses, each with, in the window, for show, an identical china ornament, the realisation of some strange ideal or perhaps, as at Pompeii, an offering to the God of Plenty; either a slouching boy, dun-coloured, with hands in his pockets, or a curtseying, winsome, small girl, in a half-crinoline, of which she holds up the ends in thick hands. Feudalism here has plainly been put a stop to, for the squire's house is a lunatic asylum, and laughter — or, if not laughter, a howling very like it — sounds continually over the well-kept lawns from where the lunatics play happily their innocent games of 'Smash the Sane Man' and 'Hunt the Warder' under the starred syringa bushes and fat-leaved, toad-speckled laurels. The Rectory is to become a Youth Hostel, or even a Civic Centre, and loud-speakers will be erected for teaching compulsory crooning at every street corner. . . . . But I forget my trade, Dick Whittington, I was about to say when this vision of a municipal paradise I have just described impinged upon my mind and cut across my story, was a foundling, discovered one winter's night on the moor, outside the village, then still a rustic, backward place. He was adopted by a blacksmith and his wife, who brought him up as if he were their own son, providing him with a comfortable home, warm both in hearth and heart. The winter he enjoyed especially, for in the long dark afternoons, he was allowed to sit at the back of the smithy, which resembled a cave, listening to the rhythmic clanging of hammer on anvil and watching the sparks trace their comet-like path across the rectangle of dark blue sky through the doorway. All his life he remembered this, the smell of the hot iron and singed hoof, and the hammering and stamping of horses.

He was only twelve years old, however, when a great plague swept the country, carrying off the smith and his wife, so that Dick found himself back where he started in the bleak and misty darkness of Whittington Moor, a broken, wintry wood that lay south of the village, towards the big town of Chesterfield. At night the wind roared through the scrubby young beech and sycamore, and whistled through the chinks of the low, loosely built walls of dun stone. With darkness, the boy would fall asleep, but the cold wind would soon wake him, and he would lie on his coat, spread on the ground, watching the flames of Staveley Furnace, that moved like the tongues of lions, or a few sparks that flew up from the pyramid of cinders making a pattern against the sky. And this would cause him to think again of his father, rhythmically hammering, the sparks flying up from the anvil, until as he lay there, he seemed almost to hear that double sound, both sharp and bell-like. . . . There was no one to look after him, and no one for him to look after—except a small black kitten; which together with a few things placed in a bandanna handkerchief, made into a bundle and tied to his stick, formed his entire possessions. It was not easy to feed the kitten, for she would not eat berries, but he had not been able to find it in his heart to leave her behind, for she was one of the litter of the old black cat in the forge, and was all that he had now to remind him of his home. Besides, the little creature from her earliest days had adopted him.

He had started to leave without her, and on each occasion, as he had reached the outskirts of the village, he had heard a mewing, and looked round—and there she was! Twice he had gone back with her to the forge, black and deserted, so utterly dead with its strange lack of fire and clangour. But the third time he found her, he had to let her be.

The kitten was very young then, a playful little beast, resembling, when at rest, a black woollen ball; but she was usually in movement. A touch of Persian in her ancestry gave her long, more silky hair than the usual cat, and her front paws were white, and very subtile. Already, too, she was accomplished and could leap vertically in the air, to a height amazing for her size. In the daytime Dick, seated on a fallen tree trunk, would spend hours in swinging his bundle, tied to the stick, backwards and forwards, so that the kitten could jump at it, or knock it with a white paw, after watching it as if it were alive. She was so active and pretty, indeed, that strangers passing over the Moor would stop to stroke the little creature, and even dog-lovers would say—and the remark was intended as a compliment— 'She's more like a dog than a cat!' . . . But the truth was that no kitten could be more like a kitten.

Dogs, much more plainly than cats, have names attached to their personalities, because dogs are active, aggressive, belong to the business world, and move much in military circles. (Almost every officer, young or old, is followed—or led—by a dog: but few are followed by cats.) So for the most part, they bear the names of generals, though seldom of admirals or air-marshals— and, of course, of the better kind of financier. (Down, Melchett! Down, Joel!) Often too, they are styled after politicians—(Down, Attlee, down, Anthony—posterity is free to vary and modernise these labels) or bear imaginative onomatopoeic names, that might, when uttered loudly be the sound of their own barking; Spot! Smut!

Shot! Splash! Dash! Dingle! But Dick found it difficult to know what to call the kitten, until one day, a passing traveller, seeing her playing, asked him her name. Hearing that the lad had found none for her, he remarked: 'You ought to call her *Roxana*: it's a Persian name.' Liking its outlandish sound, Dick adopted the stranger's suggestion, shortening the word to *Roxy*.

One morning, in the pheasant-feathered tail of autumn, before the first snow had fallen, a crisp Derbyshire morning of cobwebs and mists and scented, golden bracken, and of red berries which—for there had been a gale—covered the path through the wood and scrunched underfoot, Dick and his kitten were setting out for London to seek their fortune. He felt sad at leaving, but the kitten stopped from time to time, to play with a red berry on the green moss, knocking it backwards and forwards, and as Dick did not wish to waste time, he put Roxy in the pocket of his coat, with just her head showing out of it, and gradually her mewing and purring comforted him, until, whistling a popular tune of the day, *Three Sailor Lads*, he began to stride along in the direction of Chesterfield, confidently, almost cheerfully.

Already he could see the crooked, crumpled spire of the church there round which, it was said, the devil had wound his tail cork-screwing its shape in front of him; but now he began to feel hungry and called at a farmhouse, that seemed so isolated in its own world of the early morning, with its sounds of lowing and braying and cackling and clucking, as to be an hallucination that by midday would vanish with the fading mists; but it proved to be substantial enough, and there he obtained a drink of milk for himself and his kitten. The farmer's wife told him, at the same time, to come to the kitchen fire and warm himself. Sitting by the fire was a carter who asked the boy what business he was on, and hearing his story, and that he was bent on going to London, where even the paving-stones, the lad had been told, were made of gold, said that he would give him a lift there. For three days they drove southward, and then, one morning, just as the winter's sun was topping the dome of St. Paul's, the good-natured carter put him down, before continuing on his way to Canterbury. Sure enough, Dick saw the gold lying in heaps and strips on the pavement; but it could not be picked up. It was a singular morning, full of the tongues of bells, which were to play so important a part in his life, as well as of this delusive golden light.

It was not long, alas! before Dick discovered how little gold was to be found—and even how little paving, except in the churchyards, where he slept of a night, above the bones of generations. The city *must* be very rich, he supposed, but there was little sign of it in the exteriors of the houses, and he never saw the inside of them, though a policeman had promised him he would see the inside of a prison. For the most part, people were so busy that when he tried to stop them to tell them his story, they merely hurried on. The carter, when he left, had given him a loaf, but that was three days ago, and for a whole day he had had nothing to eat, nor had poor Roxy, and no one had spoken to him, except the policeman of whom I've just told you, and an officer of the Prevention of Cruelty to Animals, who had come up to him, and had said that the kitten looked half-starved, and that if the boy was not careful, he would be prosecuted. Hearing this, Dick ran off as fast as his weak legs would take him. . . . That night in the churchyard, Roxy howled for the first time—hitherto, she had only mewed and purred—and this had given him an idea. The next day, he sang in the street, holding his hat in front of him. . . . Fortunately, he sang very badly, and had a loud voice, so people listened and liked his singing, as always in London streets, and gave him money—and advice. 'Don't get your voice trained whatever you do,' they advised him, 'or you'll spoil its freshness.' Even

now, however, he barely earned enough to keep himself
and Roxy.

One morning, Dick was singing outside a grand house
in a square, when a large old gentleman, standing in a
bow-window, heard him. The old gentleman remained
there for a minute or two, puffing like a whale, in the
way that large old gentlemen are apt to puff when they
stand in bow-windows. Then he turned away, and in
a moment or two had opened the door and had arrived
in the open air, under the portico. From there, with a
manner suggesting that he thought he could not be seen,
he examined the boy, very slowly, very carefully, and
when his eyes had reached as far as the kitten's black
face, peering out of the pocket of the ill-fitting jacket,
and her two white paws hanging over it from their joints,
he began to walk ponderously down the steps. Dick went
on singing. It was a rather dismal sound, he realised,
but the feel of the cold, hard pavers of the churchyard
was still in his young bones, nor had he been able to
afford breakfast.

The old gentleman, advancing towards him, had said:
'The police'll be after you, m'lad, if you go on like
that. Stop that horrible noise, can't you?'

'Please sir, I can't stop it,' Dick replied. 'I'm doing it
for my living.'

'Well, tell me your story instead.'

This Dick proceeded to do, and having heard it, the
old gentleman pronounced: 'You shall have work in my
house.'

'But I can't be separated from my cat,' Dick cried,
pointing to his kitten.

'Certainly not,' the old gentleman agreed, 'you can't
leave her. Besides she'll probably make a fine mouser.
She has the look of one to me—and there's always room
in the world for a mouser.'

Then the old gentleman took Dick into the hall, rang
the bell, and when the butler answered it, said 'Grinder!

take this lad downstairs, and tell Mrs. Grinder that first, before anything else, she's to give him, and his kitten, some breakfast. . . .I'll see her later.'

Dick had noticed how different the old gentleman's clothes were from any that he had hitherto seen: for everything he wore appeared to be of the finest material, though most sober and plainly cut. And now it turned out that he was a famous merchant. He owned a fleet of ships, and traded with Russia for sables, for drugs of Tartary, and the white furs of the Arctic Circle— where, on occasion, his ships took so great risks for him, in going to the farthest extremity of the ocean, that they are still there, fast in the ice—with India for spices and pepper, with Arabia for perfumes, with Egypt for henna, with the rest of Africa for diamonds and emeralds, and with the races of the distant isles, who grow horse-hair on their heads, for pearls; to all these places he sent in return English wool or English cloth. Mr. Fitzwarren —for that was the old gentleman's name—was a widower with one daughter, Pamela, a lovely girl of ten, but rather large for her age; indeed she was already taller than Dick by an inch or two. She had fair hair, of a darker colour than usual, brown eyes, and a thick, smooth, fair skin: but an unusual elegance attended her. She was very proud, though, and not as kind as her father, and thought it beneath her dignity even to look at Dick.

The task allotted to him was to wait on Mrs. Grinder, and since he was in her company all day in the kitchen, or within reach in the scullery, she had plenty of opportunity for finding fault with him. Indeed he was glad when night came, and he could go to bed; for he had been given a garret to himself, right at the top of the house. This bare little room had one window, opening on to the roof, and so, very convenient for Roxy. In the morning, he would have to get up at five to clear the stoke-hole and light the fires for boiler and kitchen. Mrs. Grinder would not come down till eight o'clock,

and from that time on, she would always find the opportunity to give Dick a harsh word or allot him an unplea-
sant task. For example, she would often order him to peel
the onions, so that his eyes should water. Then she
would laugh at him and call out 'Cry-baby!' She was
for ever telling him that she would poison his cat, if
the animal entered the kitchen (which she did constantly
to look for Dick). And it appeared almost as if Roxy
provoked Mrs. Grinder purposely, for the manner in
which the cat, as she grew older, caught mice almost in
defiance of Mrs. Grinder, who maintained that she herself
was so clean and economical a cook that there could be
none in the house, must have infuriated her. And Roxy,
as if to emphasise their numbers, commonly carried the
scalps of the mice to her master, laying them out in a
row on the kitchen floor, so that they could be counted
by anyone who walked through, and there could be no
gainsaying them. The cat brought them to Dick either
as a sign of her own prowess, or as a gift; but Mrs.
Grinder thought it an act of mere spite, and pretended
to think that the cat caught them in neighbouring houses.
She proceeded, therefore, to take it out of Dick in a
variety of ways. Herself, she talked Cockney and therefore liked to make fun of the boy's way of talking, for
he 'spoke broad,' as the phrase goes in Derbyshire. He
used 'Tha' and Thee,' and said 'yoursen' for 'yourselves,'
and indulged in many uncouth and rustic expressions.
In her acrid voice, Mrs. Grinder would mimic him, for
she liked to humiliate him in front of people, especially
in front of Miss Pamela, since she loved the little girl as
much as she hated Dick and Roxy. He used to hide
sometimes, so as to see the child pass, and Mrs. Grinder,
noticing this, would pretend not to be aware of it, and
then, as Miss Pamela went by, would haul him out of
his refuge, thereby making him look silly. Or if the
little girl chanced to stop for a moment to play with
Roxy—to whom she paid more attention than to Dick,

for cats are all of one class—Mrs. Grinder would call
her to order, saying, 'Naow, Miss Pamela, that dirty little
animal belongs to that dirty little boy, and isn't for the
likes of yaou to pli' with!'

Mrs. Grinder's friends alleged that she had a kind
heart, and indeed it may be so, but a kind tongue would
have been more to the purpose. Unfortunately, she prided
herself on 'always speaking out, to people's fices.' With
her, however, it took three, not two, to make a quarrel;
for, besides the person whom she assaulted, she had to
have another in whom she could confide her injuries and
triumphs. Thus, when Mrs. Grinder was having one of
her perpetual rows with other people, she would tempo-
rarily become more amiable to Dick; but he hated her
grumbling about others, almost more than her direct
abuse of himself.

She would stand at the kitchen-table, chopping, usually,
her figure looking during these moods like an old-
fashioned cottage loaf, her face fashioned, it seemed, of
one of the raw meats with which she was always dealing.
'I knaow I've got a temper,' she would say to him, 'not
one of those slaow tempers. Grinder mi' be thankful,
but you knaow, easy to raouse, easy to gaow as they si'—
but one thing I can't abide, and that's to let things gaow
on and not speak aout. I can't bear false fices, or people
'oo si' one thing to your fice and another be'ind your back.
I must 'ave it aout. Neither Grinder nor me are ones
to let things lie on us; oh, naow, not us. So I said to
Grinder, "you gaow and fetch 'er, and I'll tell her strite,
I will to 'er fice." "I shouldn't," Grinder said, "I
shouldn't, Mother; you'll only upset yourself." "I'm not
a coward, Grinder," I said, "a runner; I can look arter
myself if it comes to that!" So 'e brought 'er . . . I
didn't si' much, you knaow, I didn't let myself gaow;
I jus' said "Hemmer, yer mean, sneaky little 'aound, was
it yaou, that told Mrs. Norbury as I said Mrs. Craowker
was'n better than she should be; was it yaou, yaou dirty

cringer, yaou, speaking one thing to the fice, and another be'ind the back? Was it yaou? Aout with it," I says, like that, "Aout with it, for I like things strite and above board. If I 'ave a thing agen a person, then I si' it— but si' it about 'em, that's a thing I'd never do. Never. Neither me nor Mr. Grinder, and if Mrs. Craowker is naow better than she should be, what 'as that to do with me?" I ses. "That" she ses, very stuck up and nasty, "is what I ask myself, Mrs. Grinder." "O you 'orrible little beast" I ses, as quick as anything, "you mean 'ownd, so it was yaou! I'd be ashimed to be your mother, I would. Hemmer . . ." ' So the denunciation, the repining, would continue, sometimes for hour after hour.

At last, driven equally beyond endurance by her bad treatment of him and her nagging confidences, he determined to run away. Yet he hesitated and procrastinated because Mr. Fitzwarren had been so kind to him, and he feared it might seem ungrateful, and, in addition, a single amiable glance from Miss Pamela would make him alter his mind. At last, however, one morning after breakfast, he overheard Mrs. Grinder—who was chopping up a chicken at the time, and did not realise that he was standing in the doorway—confide in a loud voice to one of the kitchen-maids, 'I taold the Master that Dick might mike a cabin boy on one of his ships, but 'e'll never mike a footman or even a pantry boy, so the Master's only keeping 'im till the winter's aowver, because it's difficult to find another boy naow, and then 'e's sending 'im to Japan.'

When Dick heard these words, they decided him— since he had no means of telling that they were not true —and he crept out of the house, stopping neither to pack his bundle, nor even to take his stick. He ran as fast as he could, not troubling to look where he was going (what did it matter?): but after about forty minutes he became tired and pulled up. Besides, the morning was

beautiful—for that, though few people realised it, was
what it was—so beautiful that he stood still and, as he
did so, had the sense of something tremendously important about to happen to him. . . . It was eleven o'clock
on a February morning, and the winter crispness, just
touched with spring, lingered in the air, while the sun
was spreading its miser's gold along the pavement. And
though coal, which gives its dark substance to the native
mists of London and turns them into fogs, was burning
in many thousands of open grates, yet in the air there
was only a vaporous opalescence that wrapped itself like
a fleece round the sun and, seemingly, a fragrance of
wood-smoke, as though it had been blown into the great
city from many hamlets on the edge of forests.

In the deserted, paved space where Dick now found
himself, there was no one passing, no one hurrying. It
was a neglected corner, full of the feeling of other days.
Nothing stirred. . . . A hush prevailed, as if sound were
dead and with it the power of hearing: albeit this loss
appeared to strengthen other senses. He tried, under
these influences, to sum up for himself what he felt,
and why he had this so urgent intimation, derived from
the very air, of something momentous for him: but all
that he could decide was that he felt lonely. . . . And
just then, he heard a loud contented purring, and looking
down, saw Roxy scampering upon velvet paws in the
minute playground she had made for herself round his
boots, for one of the laces had come undone and trailed
on the pavement, and she was knocking the tag, and
jumping after it, and performing a thousand pretty feats
of simulation, so as to preserve in her animal mind the
fiction that it, too, was a living thing.

Dick had forgotten the very existence of his cat, but
now he took her up and stroked her, and, as he did so,
a thing occurred which he was never to forget. As if
he were watching a bud break into a perfection of flower,
of which it was impossible even to dream, all the bells

of London began to ring: bells old and bells new, hoarse
bells and bells that were shrill, bells loud-mouthed and
bells soft-singing, cracked bells and whole bells, bells
that talked of material affairs, and bells that sang of ideals
lost or realised, bells that wheezed and bells that
whispered, tolling bells and pealing bells, bells that spoke
with the voice of angels, and bells that sang from depths
to a darker vision. The air itself seemed to be of the
substance of their vibration. In after years, he wondered
whether it really could have happened, and what it could
have portended, what it signified: for, indeed, there were
no victories to celebrate except those always current in a
great city, the victory of greed over kindness, age over
youth, Dives over Lazarus, the healthy over the sick.
But why should bells ring for such ordinary triumphs
of the town. . . . Still, they *had* rung.

They rang for a full ten minutes, carillons of frost and
sun, songs that with the greatest virtuosity sang an idiot
tune. Then, suddenly, they changed in an instant, and
just as, when you are in a railway carriage, the train can
fit its rhythm to anything, sing in your ear any words
or composition it chooses, from a Beethoven symphony
to a song such as 'I do like to be beside the seaside,' so
all at once the bells sang in unison these words:

> 'Turn again, Whittington,
> Lord Mayor of London!
> Turn again, Whittington,
> You must be bold.
> Turn again, Turn again!
> Learn again, Learn again!
> Then London will bring you
> Your streets paved with gold.'

On hearing this message, so strangley delivered, Dick
returned to Mr. Fitzwarren's house, and when his master
sent for him, and inquired why he had run away, the boy
told him the truth, saying how cruelly he had been treated

in the kitchen. In consequence, Mr. Fitzwarren spoke severely to Mrs. Grinder, and she never thereafter held him up to ridicule, or gave him cause for complaint.

*   *   *   *

When Dick was fifteen or sixteen, Mr. Fitzwarren, who always liked to share his good fortune with those working for him, called together the members of his household, to inform them that a ship of his was sailing in a few days for a distant country, and that reason and experience led him to believe that this enterprise would be especially rewarding in its results. If, therefore, any of his servants cared to put money into the venture, or, if their savings were insufficient, to confide to the hands of the ship's Captain, objects that he could sell on their behalf at great profit to the natives, they were free to do so. All the servants gave him their thanks for his kindness, and until the vessel started, talked of little else but this coming gamble. Even Mrs. Grinder abandoned her usual subjects of conversation, in order to talk of it, though in different vein from the rest.

'It's just a trick,' she said, as she larded a bit of meat. 'It's just a trick of the Master's,' she repeated in a voice loud enough to stand out against a background of sizzling, 'a wi of getting our sivings, as 'e can't get 'em any other wi, so as to keep us servants. It's because 'e knows in 'is 'eart that one man's as good as another.'

Mrs. Grinder, however, did not really herself believe what she said, and was as excited as the rest. A pleased air of expectancy obtained. The most thrifty of the household brought money to Mr. Fitzwarren to invest in the enterprise, but the rest of them brought their most precious possessions: for example, housemaids and kitchenmaids brought such things as a filagree box, sent from India by a sailor-cousin, a pincushion in puce velvet with *Dinna Ken*, or some Scottish motto of that sort, inscribed on it in false seed pearls, a turquoise brooch consisting of a spider's bulbous body caught in its own web of golden threads—or were they legs?—a matchbox of Dutch silver, with a pattern on the top that human eye could never unravel, a china figure, of mat surface, but eruptive, that represented an idealisation of 1880 charm, all flounces, smiles and frills, an alarum clock, of some grievous white metal, through which showed a yellow core, its bells worn at the jaunty angle to which the years had knocked it, a china box with a fox terrier painted on it, the poor little creature's head very much on one side, as though a stroke had interposed, giving to a mood of intense and foolish inquisitiveness a temporary permanence, a silver photograph frame embossed with a design of tulips, and a cushion, black silk one side, and white on the other, with painted on it in water-colour, a vivid, realistic design of red poppies. Everyone brought something, money or personal chattels, all except Dick. Alone of the whole household, he had no savings and no belongings with which he could part. Thus, while the others were talking cheerfully of what the vessel would bring them on the return voyage, Dick, dispirited and humiliated, would sit in his garret, with his cat for sole company.

His idea came to him only just in time. One afternoon, as the household gathered on the steps to give a send-off to the Captain, who had been having luncheon with his employer, and was now starting to go down to the docks, Dick, who was at the back, broke through the little knot of people, with Roxy asleep in his arms, and cried to Mr. Fitzwarren:

'I have nothing of my own, Sir, nothing to sell, except this cat. She is all I have to make my fortune. Please take her, Sir, and ask the Captain to sell her for me.'

At this the cat—she was now full grown, though of slight stature—struggled to escape; but her master handed her over to Mr. Fitzwarren, and he passed her on to the Captain. She now remained still and quiet, but, sitting up on the Captain's arms, gazed at Dick, while two large tears, that glittered like diamonds (but they were *not* diamonds or Roxy would have been retained at home), formed in her eyes. It was, indeed, an affecting scene, and much impressed all those who were there, even Mrs. Grinder. Miss Pamela cried, and her father warmly congratulated the boy on his spirit of enterprise, and above all, of self-sacrifice. And a Mr. MacMagnus, a close friend of Mr. Fitzwarren's, and a master of industry, who had also been present at the luncheon, exclaimed, so that everyone could hear it, 'That young man will go far.' Since Mr. MacMagnus possessed a reputation for spotting coming men, these words produced all the more effect.

The Captain, still clasping Roxy in his arms, climbed into the waiting cab, and as it drove away, the master of the house, Miss Pamela, Mr. MacMagnus and the cluster of servants, waved their hands and cheered. Roxy still made no effort to escape, but even above the rattling of the wheels and the cheering, could be heard her sobbing. But it did not reach Dick, for in his head rang bells that sang:

> 'Turn again, Turn again!'
> 'Learn again, Learn again!'

* * * *

Time began to move more quickly, for Dick was growing up. He was much more popular in the house now. For one thing, it was generally felt that his giving the cat away like that showed that there was something to him, and proved that he possessed both character and acumen. And, in itself, the absence of the cat made life easier for him. Mrs. Grinder, for example, no longer bore him a grudge, had even come to like him. And everyone in the house seemed now to value his society because of his cheerfulness, for the truth was that in the two years that had elapsed since Mr. Fitzwarren had last heard of his ship, the whole household had grown depressed: for them, so much was at stake.

At last a message reached Mr. Fitzwarren that the vessel was still lying loaded in the harbour of Nebaka-Koko, the chief port of Tongador, and, worse, that a great plague was sweeping over the country. Many began to fear that the Captain and his crew were dead, and that, in consequence, they would lose or had lost, all they possessed—but Dick had only lost his cat, if that were so, and he thought little about the matter.

It must have been two or three years after the ship had left England, when Dick had almost reached manhood, that one night—he still slept in the garret—he woke up with a start. A full moon shone through the open window, showing a world of roofs. He thought the cold must have woken him, for it was a very frosty night, but then, he heard a mewing, and with a tremendous bound, a black cat leapt lithely across the sill and landed on his bed. . . . Well, it was odd, though there was nothing particularly surprising in it, he supposed—but as the animal raised her body, the moon caught it, and he saw that this particular cat fairly blazed with jewels; which *was* a little surprising. At first Dick thought he must be dreaming. The cat stood, arching its back, in a flood of light from the moon. A small dog-collar of enormous brilliants surrounded its throat, though the long, silky Persian hair a little obscured their scintillation. What appeared to be a single, huge emerald sparkled from the left ear, being inset there after the Hindu fashion, and round the right fore paw glittered an anklet of rubies. But this could be no dream, for the cat came straight to Dick, and, as he sat up in bed, jumped on his shoulder, and rubbed its head against his neck.

It *was* Roxy, there could be no doubt about it. She purred loudly, and after a few minutes, climbed down from Dick's shoulder on to the bed, and sat there, looking at him, and scratching at her neck with a paw, as

if she wanted something. After a while Dick understood:
she wanted him to undo the clasp for her and take
the necklace off. That done, the cat stretched itself
beside him, and slept.

The next day, the Captain, who proved to have survived all the dangers of the voyage, came to luncheon,
and afterwards sent for Dick, to tell him of his good
fortune, and how it happened.

When the ship had arrived at Nebaka-Koko, the great
white plague was at its height. The negroes called it
The White Death. Everything was deserted; every being,
every living thing in some of the vast, teeming cities,
seemed to be dead. As the ship drew into the harbour,
into the atmosphere of the shore, where the torrid African
heat danced in a sultry confusion above beach and houses
and grounds, the crew had been amazed to see no bathers,
no boatmen, no loungers, no longshoremen even—only an
army of skeletons that balefully glittered. The fever and
heat had driven whole crowds down to the sea, to try
and cool their simmering blood. Some had died as they
entered the water, others where they stood or reclined,
under the vultures, watching how they might descend to
enforce equality, to prove that the black races, too,
possessed the whitest of skeletons. So this great multitude
of the dead reclined among the enormous shells, thick-
lipped shapes in nacre that are to be found on tropical
shores, or stood out against a background of gardens, of
trellised arbours and arches in the Moorish manner, and
colonnades round which twined the serpentine branches
of the unfamiliar plants of the country, now expanding
their huge orange and purple cups. The few black faces
that remained from the plague, seemed to have a green
shutter of fear over them; their eyes peeped out from the
arches, rolling, as if in search of comfort. Even the
whites of the eyes now had this green light in them.

Nor had it been any better in Ta-Balu, the capital, the
great city. Few of the inhabitants dared to move out of

their houses, though the gaily-coloured streets of mud, and the chattering market-places were silent, shuddering in the white blaze of noon. Here and there a venomous serpent, escaped from the snake-charmers who had fallen dead in the chief piazza during the climax of their most ingenious tricks, hissed from a gutter, and the lions, now free of keepers, could be seen shaking their manes and trotting back with heraldic gait to their homes in the Central Forest.

Even now, though so many had already perished, the plague had increased in virulence. Day by day, those still living fell dead, as they walked, were carried in litters, or drove; at the sides of the roads, in the ditches, the corpses lay, piled up, where they had tumbled as they contracted the sickness. And then it approached the precincts of *Mon Repos*, the Mountain Palace, where the Emperor, crowned and wearing his robes of State, and clasping the two-edged Sword of Justice in his hand, sat trembling in the innermost court. The corridors and galleries, with their vast arches open to snare the winds, though usually full of courtiers and officials, were now empty: those who remained alive no longer wished to walk there, to catch the tainted air. Besides superstition held—and science supported it—that the plague was borne by rats, and His Majesty himself had heard the sound of them, that increased noticeably from day to day in the galleries as he walked. And sometimes, when the Emperor felt so fearful of the creatures that he climbed to the top of the great tower, where, surely, he would be secure from them, even there, as he looked down on the vast and glistening expanse of the African champaign, with its groves of orange that held under their leaves a perpetual night, dark and balmy, that was lit only by their fruit, with its hedges of pomegranate and its fields of mangoes and melons and paw-paws, he would see the furrows filled with an advancing army of horrid black shapes, all, it seemed to him, hurrying towards the palace. What could he do?

First he sent for the witch of the white people, the Rodent Officer of the Agricultural Control Board, lately inaugurated, through Geneva, by the white powers. She was a fat American woman, who wore a green Rodent Officer's coat, and blue serge trousers, inappropriate to her structure. She had a lighted cigarette stub, clipped to her upper lip all the time she worked or talked. Having surveyed *Mon Repos* and its grounds, she put down two powders, a white and a black, to destroy the rats. On it they throve, and their progeny pullulated. Evidently word of the delicacies she had provided spread quickly, for the rats seemed to double the size of their armies in a day, as well as to increase noticeably in stature. Next the Emperor summoned a witch-doctor from a far province of his empire: she arrived, clad in veils, and cowrie-shells, anointed her enormous body with a special sacred unguent, and danced wildly in every chamber of the palace. Still the rats survived, though she was executed. Then dried herbs were burnt; but still the rats poured in from all directions. Then the most sacred relics were fetched from Ta-Balu, in procession, to the beating of drums made of human skin. Yet the whole country, when seen from the Tower of the Sun, seemed to be moving—and moving centripetally, in one direction.

The Emperor was growing desperate. As he sat in state on his throne of gold in the Hall of the Royal Fetishes — a great apartment hung with countless Venetian mirrors, one above another, spread haphazard over the walls, the many recesses of which each contained the immense skeleton of a brass bedstead—it seemed to him that the palace was almost empty save for the rats. The mirrors and the polished brass balls of the bedsteads reflected nothing but his own royal countenance; even the pages, in their scarlet liveries and white wigs, which made their faces look still more black, were fewer; they had

' gone away '—for nobody must mention death to the
Emperor. His courtiers *went away*, they never died.
The mirrors, then, showed endless vistas of other mirrors,
of a dusty, flyblown pomp. The sound characteristic of
the palace had become, no longer the throbbing of drums,
but the bumping and squeaking of the rats.

From the Hall of the Royal Fetishes the Emperor
issued a proclamation that promised a great fortune to
any living thing that would destroy the rats. He waited:
alas, no slightest diminution of the scuffling occurred—
and then, one noon, as he was returning for luncheon
from the Hall, through the Great Coronation Corridor
of the Golden Wind, as it was called, he saw, laid out
with military precision in a long row, stretching from
the door to the first of the open arches, the bodies of
151 rats. After the preliminary and instinctive shudder
that the sight evoked, the Emperor was, of course, highly
delighted. He looked everywhere around him, to see who
was responsible for the massacre, but there seemed to be
no one present—then, as his eyes searched every possible
corner, to his surprise he observed a black cat leap out
from hiding, and race along the gallery, until like
a tiger it pounced on another black body. Soon the
little cat, for it was not a large animal, returned down
the middle of the corridor, and boldly placed at His
Majesty's feet the burden it was dragging along, a large,
black rat, hardly smaller than itself. The Emperor, much
impressed, clapped his hands, and ordered a bowl of
zebra's milk to be brought immediately, so that the cat,
his champion, should be able to recruit his strength—
and before many weeks had passed, Roxana—for it was
she—had killed or driven out by intimidation every rat
from the palace, from the mountain, and from the sur-
rounding plain. In consequence, the plague abated.

It had happened in this way — Mr. Fitzwarren had
charged the Captain of his vessel to deliver in person a
present to the Emperor, together with a letter. Finding,

when he arrived at Nebaka-Koko that the Court had already left Ta-Balu for *Mon Repos,* accordingly, he rode on in that direction, taking the cat with him. Once Roxy had seen a rat, there was no holding her; her fortune was made—and made it certainly was. For not only did the Emperor decree that a temple was to be built to her, not only did he confer on her the title *Lion Champion and Court Sacred Whisker,* but he bestowed upon her a sack filled with uncut jewels of great value. In addition, he ordered a large emerald to be cut for her ear, and a few weeks later gave an audience—it was safe now to receive people in the palace—to all the foreign ambassadors, and native dukes, and in front of them, as a mark of the imperial favour, had himself clasped the diamond dog-collar round the cat's neck, while the band of the Assassin Guard, dressed in their ceremonial uniform of leopard skins, and high open-work crowns made of human ribs, thumped and brayed in unison a march by Sousa. And further, as final proof of his pleasure, and in order to ensure Roxana's comfort in the future, the Emperor, after inquiring the name of her English master, dispatched to 'Mr. Whittington' as that potentate styled him, by means of Mr. Fitzwarren's ship, an immense treasure consisting of gold and jewels, rare African drugs and the tusks of elephants, together with an invitation to accompany Roxana back to *Mon Repos* the following summer, and spend some months there.

Eventually, as Dick could see for himself, the ship had arrived safely home. No sooner though, had she been brought to anchor, than the cat, flouting the orders of the Captain and defying the Customs House and the Quarantine officials, had climbed a mast, and, taking a superb leap for the shore, had gone straight home to Dick. Two days later the cargo was unloaded, and the treasure that Roxy had brought Dick proved far to surpass in value the rest of the contents of the ship. Mr. Fitzwarren nevertheless maintained his reputation as a just man, in no way showing disappointment, but on the contrary congratulating Dick and advising him how to invest his fortune. Moreover his generous-minded master promised to find the young man—he was now eighteen —a place in his office. Indeed, everyone, since the news of his good fortune, had formed a high opinion of his character and capacities, and Mr. MacMagnus, who had been the first to divine his latent talents, and who was again present, pronounced this time, as he watched the cargo being carried off the vessel:

'That young man has made good!'

When summer came, Mr. Fitzwarren gave Dick permission to accept the Emperor's invitation, and to take Roxy out to Tongador. The country had completely recovered its customary prosperity, and Dick and his cat were immensely fêted in whatever part of the Empire they travelled. They spent several happy months in *Mon Repos*, and Roxy was very contented on the whole, for she was nearly always in the company of her master. She would sit at his side for hours, by one of the open arches of the Great Coronation Corridor, where first she had made his fortune, watching the birds dip and swing over the brooding summer plain, carolling and turning as if to tempt her. Only then would she become a little restless, making a curious deep sound, mingled of fury and calculation, in her throat, while she measured with cocked eye the distance between her and the spire of the nearest cypress, which, though its scent was wafted so strongly thither, could not be attained. And again, now that there were no rats to hunt in the palace, she missed the regular exercise; so evidently, that, since the Emperor had appointed to the cat her own slaves, they would occasionally arrange a hunt for her for the day in some outlying portion of the royal domain. Even for these pleasures, she disliked—and showed it plainly—having to be parted from her master, albeit for so short a time.

Fortunately during these expeditions Dick was at no

loss to find employment: for business constituted his
chief interest, and he had brought it with him. Because
Mr. MacMagnus had found an opportunity of speaking
to him before he left, and had said:

'You know, my boy, I have your interests at heart.
They're very backward out there, where you're going. . . .
Now, don't say a word about it to dear old Fitz, he's a
dear old fellow, though so antiquated in his ways, but
take out some models of good modern stuff to show the
Emperor; you know, the things that make modern
countries, and make them great, Bren guns, tanks, flame-
throwers. He's sure to be interested. I'll supply the
models, and if you are successful, I will make it worth
your while.'. . . When the Emperor saw the toys, he was,
naturally, delighted and ordered a great many of the
originals of each model from Mr. MacMagnus. And
already, before Dick had left the country, he had been
able to see for himself some of the benefits resulting from
his enterprise: for the Emperor had no sooner obtained
the articles—and they, together with the bills, had been
delivered with a praiseworthy promptitude—that, in order
to pay for them, he declared war on the neighbouring
State of Kobalola. It was rather difficult to do, because
the moral reasons for a war had to be thought out quickly,
and the Emperor, being an absolute monarch, had to
carry out this difficult work for himself. However, he
soon issued a moving proclamation:

'Our patience' it read, 'is exhausted. We have long
had no aim except to live in peace, only with that purpose
in view has our great and unconquerable army been
built up. This power we never dreamt of using, until
the atrocities of the enemy, committed upon our allies,
the Race of the South, compelled us to submit our sword
to the dread arbitrament of war. We shall proceed
resolutely and unflinchingly towards our goal, to widen
the world basis of Democracy, and institute a reign of
peace in Kobalola.'

It can be imagined with what a burst of cheering the people of Tongador welcomed the inspiring sentiment and close reasoning of this document. The warriors fought with more than their accustomed bravery, and before many days had elapsed, the Emperor had entered the enemy capital. Here, Dick and Roxy joined His Majesty, in order to be present at the ceremonies that marked the Peace Treaty. This exacted a large indemnity—or tribute as it used to be called—from the defeated power. And Dick, being, as Mr. MacMagnus had comprehended, an enterprising young man, was able to book a larger order from the ruler of it, for machines similar to those employed by the Emperor, but of an improved type.

*   *   *   *

When Dick returned to London, Mr. MacMagnus was delighted at the manner in which someone so new to business had carried out the suggested transactions. Moreover, divining the real nature of the young man's genius, he now proposed that, while Dick should remain a further two years with Mr. Fitzwarren so as to learn the details of the business, some of which, it appeared, were secret, he should, at the end of that period, leave him. Mr. MacMagnus would, in the meantime, found two new concerns, one connected with the making of armaments, the other, of the same kind as Mr. Fitzwarren's, and on Dick joining him, and bringing him the benefit of his experience, he would be made a partner in both. Dick, who, as he used to say, was determined 'to be beholden to nobody,' felt that this was an offer he could not afford to refuse—besides, he wished soon to be in a position to propose marriage to Pamela, with whom he was more than ever in love, and he certainly could not expect her to throw herself away on a poor man.... For the present, Mr. MacMagnus and Dick both agreed that it would better to say nothing of their plans, for fear of competition.

Things now began to prosper with Dick, and this state itself helped to intensify his run of fortune. Everyone agreed how much he had improved. He had quite shed his old roughness, both of speech and conduct, and was a typical young business man, as smart in his appearance as in the bargains he struck. It would have been difficult to tell that he was not a Londoner bred. Mrs. Grinder now always addressed him as 'Sir,' when she saw him, and consulted him, rather than Mr. Fitzwarren, about her own small affairs. As for Pamela, she had begun to return his affection, and Mrs. Grinder now did everything she could to further the match. At the end of two years, when, as arranged with Mr. MacMagnus, Dick picked a quarrel with Mr. Fitzwarren and walked out of the office, Pamela took the part of the young man. Her father was very angry with him at first, but then, as Mrs. Grinder said to Pamela, 'You won't mind my siying it, Miss Pamela, but 'e's getting past it. Hit's time 'e retired.' And, indeed, his luck had deserted him, and he had lost much money. On the whole, the world took Dick's side. Indeed, they thought him still further improved. And, before long Dick bought a house of his own—it happened to be the same mansion in which Mr. Fitzwarren had lived in the days of his prosperity.

The cat still followed Dick everywhere, and, when the went to dinner-parties, she had to be locked up, to prevent her escaping, and then hiding outside, or, if possible, entering the house, there lurking unobtrusively in a corner, until the moment came when she could safely make an effective sortie, leaping up, on to the middle of the dinner-table. He was, of course, still very much attached to her—they were such old companions—but, he could not help feeling a little ashamed on these occasions. Not, he had to admit to himself, that she ever upset anything when she jumped. No, it was not that. 'But, after all,' as he remarked one day to Pamela, 'I mean to say, one doesn't want a cat dogging one's footsteps all the time—if it *were* a dog, it would be different.'

Pamela agreed with him. 'You can't let it go on for ever,' she advised. 'Some time you'll *have* to put a stop to it, and force her to stay at home.'

In fact, though Dick had never been at a public school, his feelings resembled those of a boy, upon some local occasion of festivity, shocked by the non-conformity of his parents' clothes or conduct. Worse still, the sight of the cat revived old stories. And though Dick was proud of having made his own way—and never ceased to say so—neither he nor Pamela liked to be reminded of it by others. They preferred to administer it as a shock, themselves, to those whom they met—and, at any rate, what had the cat got to do with it?

Yet, though Dick began to dread Roxy's sudden emergence, there was, he had to admit to himself, nothing unusual now in the cat's appearance. If she would only stay there and watch him, instead of claiming his acquaintance so openly, not much harm would be done. Nobody would notice. She merely looked a rather old cat—she had begun to age. He had long ago removed the diamonds and rubies—not because they struck an *outré* note (though, indeed, they did), but in case any thief should see them, and trap and kill the cat for their value. They were now in safe custody in the bank in his own name. The emerald was the last jewel the cat retained, but about the time that Pamela became engaged to him, she had pointed out that the emerald, by its weight, might damage the cat's ear.

'What a lovely ring it would make!' she had added, no doubt hardly thinking of what she was saying.

The engagement was not a long one, for Mr. Fitzwarren had lost his fortune owing to increased competition in his business, and Pamela did not wish to be a burden on him. All his flair for his work seemed to have deserted him, and he had grown into a very old man. At the same time, she hardly liked, when she married, to leave him to look after himself, so she gave him a flat in Dick's house. It was so convenient for him —he knew the place so well—and yet this was the part of it he had known least, so he wouldn't grow tired of it. There were practically no stairs, and servants today did not like stairs—or basements (not that he had any servants, but still it made it more modern, convenient, and 'homey'), and so Pamela had suggested that the basement should be made into a separate flat for him, all of his own. The old gentleman seemed happy there; at any rate he troubled no one—and everyone agreed what a thoughtful, considerate daughter he had. He was lucky—not every daughter was like that nowadays. And when Pamela and Dick went out of an evening to dine, or to the play, it was pleasant for them to know that they could leave the cat with someone they could trust. Indeed, Mr. Fitzwarren liked having the little creature with him, for he seldom went out or saw anyone. Even Mr. MacMagnus, when he came to dine with the young people upstairs, used to declare that it would make him too sad to see Mr. Fitzwarren as he was now, he'd been so different in the dear old days—still, of course, he'd go down at once and see him if it would do him any good or help him, but it wouldn't! The old gentleman, on the occasion when Mr. MacMagnus—who was only three years younger—had gone to visit him, had hardly seemed to recognise his old friend, and was very glum. It would only unsettle him again, they agreed. So Mr. Fitzwarren and Roxy would sit together through the long winter evenings, staring into the fire. She seldom escaped—though, of course, twice she contrived to sneak away to a house where Dick and Pamela were dining, and on one occasion to appear on the ledge of their box at a musical comedy. On the whole, however, everything proceeded happily until Pamela, who for a long time had been saying 'Dick, you really *ought* to have a dog,' gave him, on his birthday, an Irish terrier called Pat. Then there was no holding Roxy; she knew about it long before she saw the dog—indeed before the dog had arrived at the house. She refused all milk, and even fish, and would not take any nourishment at all. Further, she arched her back, hissed and spat at her best friends. And she managed to get out of the basement flat and attack her rival without any provocation, scratching his eyes, and ripping his left ear from top to bottom; a mark which poor Pat carried to the end of his days.

For the cat's own sake, this sort of thing could not be allowed to continue. Pamela felt it her duty to speak to Dick about it.

'You ought to give the creature away to someone who lives in the country,' she said, 'She'd be far happier; and all that jumping on the table makes *you* look so unusual. After all, *I* get the blame: I married you—and like every good wife, I want my husband to be just the same as other men—only richer, of course.'

'Darling, I promise to find someone to look after her later on. But I don't like to give her away. I don't know why.'

'It's all very well for you. You don't hear the talk. It's not nice for me—people bring out the whole story of your coming to London, and say that I've married beneath me. And that I know that I have done so, doesn't make it any better!'

'Darling, please don't say such hard things!!'

'But you oughtn't to put up with it. You ought to show more respect for your wife. . . . Besides, it would be kinder to the cat herself.'

'She looks quite well—though we hardly ever see her, really, do we?'

'You should send her right away—otherwise it'll be the same thing all over again. You don't see the sort of stir that goes round, when she appears. You complain that it makes *you* look a fool, but what about me?'

'I didn't say so, darling: you said it.'

'Please don't interrupt and contradict me, Dick, when we're talking of serious matters.'

At the moment, though, Pamela saw she could accomplish nothing. It was better to wait. So she put up with the cat until one day it got upstairs, into the drawing-room and hid there. Some friends had come to see her, and after tea they asked her to play the piano to them. She had begun to give them her favourite Chopin Prelude, and was almost in the middle of it, when Roxy, from her place of concealment, howled in so loud, piercing and heart-rending a tone, that Pamela had been obliged to stop. *That*, she realised, *had* made her look silly: she could not go on. . . . In fact, not only was Roxy damaging Dick, she was a nuisance in the house.

Next time she approached the matter more softly, more obliquely.

'Darling,' she said to her husband one morning, 'Daddy's beginning to look such an old crock now, I'm sure country air is what he needs! It would do him *so* much good, and after all he is my father! So I've asked Tickle and Galbraith to look out for a cottage in Cornwall. It's such a wonderful climate, they say. . . . Only he mustn't be allowed to feel lonely at his age, so I thought we could send Roxy down too, to keep him company—then he'll be quite happy.'

As she had hoped, Dick fell in with this plan.... But the truth of the matter was, the cat was getting beyond herself. Even in the taxi on her way to the station, she scratched and roared inside her hamper like a tiger. In the station, it was worse—and no sooner had she arrived than she was back again. How she made the distance from Cornwall to London in the time, it was impossible to imagine! She hadn't arrived at the cottage till past midnight—but the very next evening, when Pamela and Dick had gone out to dine with Lord and Lady Nuggett (he was head of the great cartel which had recently been formed with the object of helping backward countries to become forward), there was a sudden commotion, and Roxy leapt like a steeplechaser over the extended arm of the footman, who was in the act of offering a gold platter to the chief guest, into the middle of the table, just in front of Dick. . . . Naturally, the story revived. Even Dick began to feel more strongly about Roxy's behaviour. One didn't want the whole thing raked up again.

Worse still, the cat proved to have become a thief. Usually Pamela wore the emerald ring, but one day, when she was not wearing it, and when the cat had come up to London secretly, Pamela, herself unseen, observed the animal deliberately go up to the jewel-box—which was unlocked—open it with teeth and paws, and then try to sneak off, carrying the wonderful gem in her mouth. When Pamela attempted to take it away, she fought like a fury. Fortunately, Dick was near, and directly he spoke to the cat, she gave it up quietly and lay on her back, as if she expected him to play with her.

The next day, Pamela, who had been for some time considering the whole matter of the cat, tried a new line of approach, and a new plan.

'Richard,' she said—she had begun to call him Richard by now, it was such a much nicer name, she thought, than Dick—'Richard, you're so fond of cats, I wonder you don't start an almshouse for old cats. It would do so much good—and you're rich enough to afford it now. They've done a lot for you, you know, in your career: now it is up to you to do something for them. It would help to raise the whole status of the cat in society. And your cat, dear little Roxy—I've grown so fond of her— could be the first there, with a really good endowment policy. She's growing old now, and deserves to be properly looked after. I'm afraid she's not really happy with Daddy in Cornwall, or she'd stay down there, and not try so often to get away—and it shows too, that he can't exercise proper supervision. Perhaps she'd be more contented in London again. And it will be easier for other cat-lovers if the home is built here.... And I've found such a nice capable man to organise everything. He's had a great deal of experience, and is thoroughly reliable.... He was a warder at Dartmoor for a long time.'

The idea appealed to Dick. Within the space of a year, *The Whittington Central Cats' Aid Society and Sanatorium*—about which you asked me—was completed at great expense.

But, as Lady Whittington (Dick was now Sir Richard, having entered on his first term of office as Lord Mayor of London) pointed out, it would not be fair for him to have to find *all* the money for the charity, even though it had been his idea, and he was so wealthy now. He must remember that he had done it in honour of Roxy, and, after all, the cat was a rich cat. Luckily, for once he was prepared to listen to reason, and sold some of the animal's jewels to defray part of the cost of the home. . . . The details of it had been thought out with the greatest care, and one well could see why it had cost so much money. There was a proper staff of attendants provided, and each cat—but at first there was only one cat in the building—had its own comfortable cage and chain.

Unfortunately, within a week of the Sanatorium being opened—and it had been done most discreetly, without any flourish in the Press, for as Lady Whittington used to say, 'Publicity would spoil the spirit of the thing, somehow'—Roxy escaped, hid in a crowd, and took a flying leap out of it and in at the window of the Lord Mayor's coach, as it passed during one of his civic progresses. It now became impossible to keep the news of the Lord Mayor's charitable deed quiet any longer, for the attendants, who had been given very strict orders to guard the cat that day, in their anxiety to secure the animal, came running and pushing helter skelter through the jostling onlookers, who pressed together and lined the pavement behind the police.   Of course the Press took up the story.

'CAT BRINGS FORTUNE TO LORD MAYOR!'

'GRATEFUL LORD MAYOR FOUNDS CATS' HOME.'

'THE ROMANCE OF A CITY CAT.'

'A LORD MAYOR WHO LOVES CATS.'

'STORY OF PENNILESS BOY AND CAT WHO BROUGHT HIM FORTUNE.'

'FROM MANSION-HOUSE TO CATS' HOME.'

These were some of the regrettably sensational headings.

Each time the cat slipped its collar, the story grew. Londoners never tired of it. There was no peace for the Lord Mayor. At night, in his immense four-poster bed at the Mansion-House, Sir Richard would lie awake for hours. The fire burning in the grate would throw the shadows of the plumes that crowned the bed upon the wall; sometimes it would show palm trees, then the shadows would flutter and coalesce back into chaos, and reform themselves, of a sudden, into the momentary likeness of a gigantic black cat, glaring at him. He would be wide awake again, and no sooner had he with the greatest difficulty at last got to sleep, than a gentle mewing would wake him—and there would be Roxy! ... It used to distress Lady Whittington even more, to think of the cat, at her age, out in the cold night like that! And how she contrived her sudden disappearances from the Home, it was difficult to make out; for windows and doors were shut and bolted, and a fire was kept burning —so she could not have got up the chimney. No attendants, no bribes of milk or mice, no iron bars, could keep her away from Sir Richard Whittington.

The Whittingtons now placed all their hopes in a new idea—in *The Cats' Charterhouse* that, at Lady Whittington's suggestion, Sir Richard had decided to found in Gloucestershire, in the grounds of his own country house, so that his wife could herself, from time to time, keep an eye on the place and see that the cats were comfortable.... But it was no use. The instant Dick came to London, Roxy appeared too, and so old and mangy now, so gaunt and prophetic in her look, that it was difficult to recognise in her the purring black kitten that once she had been. You could almost hear the animal's bones creak as she jumped.... Next, Sir Richard and his wife began to deceive themselves with hopes of the new *Cats' Provident Society Almshouse* in the Outer Hebrides. Surely, there Roxana would be content to rest, appalled by the length and difficulties of her journey.... But not at all! This time she turned up at a small dinner-party at the Mansion-House, her fur still wet as the hair of the Old Man of the Sea from her long swim. It was fortunate that they were in their own house. The cat was captured and sent back, under an escort of warders, to her island home and several of them dismissed. So it went on, and naturally, the matter was often referred to, in the Press, and by the world in general.

The worst scandal of all was undoubtedly that of which I told you at the beginning, and which happened during Sir Richard's third term as Lord Mayor, at the inaugural Guildhall Banquet. You will remember that we left Lady Whittington giving a tactful and ingenious interview to the members of the Press. She had explained the medical causes of her husband's fainting, and had stated forthrightly, that he owed his rise in the world to his own exertions, and not to the help of any cat.

'It is just one of those silly stories that so easily gain currency in times of stress,' she added, 'no one knows *how*. And though ordinarily, I should treat it as too unimportant a matter to waste my breath over, I ought, perhaps, to deny it for the children's sake.' And then she proceeded to supply quite plausible explanations of how these tales had originated. 'In my opinion,' she continued, 'it is due chiefly to ignorance. Even today few people, comparatively, speak French—and still fewer spoke it thirty years ago. But Sir Richard in his early days travelled a good deal and spoke French fluently. Talking it so well, he became fond of the language, and it was one of his ways as a young man, even when speaking English, to introduce frequently a French word or phrase. And so, when strangers used to ask him "To what do you attribute your great success?" my husband has often, in my hearing, answered "In the first place to *achat*"—or, in plain English, "to purchases." These people, knowing no French, and consequently misunderstanding what he said, would go away and tell their friends "Whittington himself told me he owed his fortune to a *chat,* or cat." In a similar fashion, certain persons eager for sensation, and ready to seize on any evidence for the manufacture of a story—and you gentlemen of the Press know that such persons can always be found —have twisted to their purpose something else my husband used to say. In the course of building up the great industry that my husband and Lord MacMagnus founded, it was necessary for the firm to acquire its own mines, round Newcastle in point of fact, and to have its own fleet of ships to bring the coal south. For this purpose, my husband found the most convenient vessel to be a Norwegian type called in that language, a *cat.* Accordingly the fleet of ships was called cats. And often, when I've visited Sir Richard at the works, I've heard him make some remark like this: 'I've been waiting for my cat all day,' or 'I can't think what we should do without our cat! ... *Those* are the cats of which you talk! And in the same way, there's that stupid tale of a cat having brought him a fortune from the negroes! That is due to the sailors on the colliers having black faces from the coal dust. ... Except the cats of which I've told you, I know of no cat in my husband's life.

Just as she said this, while the words were still on her lips, a scratching sounded at the door of the room, and the journalist I have already had cause to mention, opened it before Lady Whittington could stop him. A cat—plainly the same that had been seen previously at the Banquet—dashed in, looked round, and then fled out again, and up the stairs to her master's bedroom, where he lay, under his plumed canopy, more seriously ill than his wife realised.

He died a rich man. But it was found that by some strange freak, he had altered his will, only a few days before his death, and had left his whole enormous fortune to the maintenance of his various cats' homes. Lady Whittington had to part with her jewels, and passed the remaining years of her life in seclusion in her late father's cottage in Cornwall. She seemed, as she grew older, to become a very ordinary old lady, except that her neighbours noticed how fiercely, even though she was now rather infirm, she would shoo away any cat that strayed into the garden or attempted to enter the house.

As for Roxana, she was never seen again. Some say she was poisoned, and that the Lord Mayor's State Bedroom at the Mansion-House is haunted by her spectre, though others maintain that this loyal and gifted cat, after her master's decease, made her way back to the scene of her former splendours, ending her life in *Mon Repos* as the honoured guest of the Emperor. But this second report does not seem to me altogether likely, for Sir Richard's great business capacity and enterprise had been responsible for supplying every kingdom in those regions with the most advanced weapons of modern warfare, and, by the time each of these countries had given the rest a New Order, and had then liberated one another, it is not to be supposed that many dwellings, many Emperors—or many subjects—were left. . . . And the most glorious war of all, the Crusade for the Lowest Common Denominator, was still to come. But, at least, it has been stated in the last few weeks by reputable travellers that the Temple the Emperor raised to Roxana still stands unscathed in the remote mountains of Tongador.